MGM'S
TOM and JERRY'S
PARTY

TOLD BY STEFFI FLETCHER

PICTURES BY M-G-M CARTOONS

ADAPTED BY

HARVEY EISENBERG AND SAMUEL ARMSTRONG

GOLDEN PRESS
Western Publishing Company, Inc.
Racine, Wisconsin

IT WAS Cook's night out. She buttoned on her coat and put on her good black hat. She threw one last look around the kitchen.

Everything was spic and span. Everything was in its place—she thought!

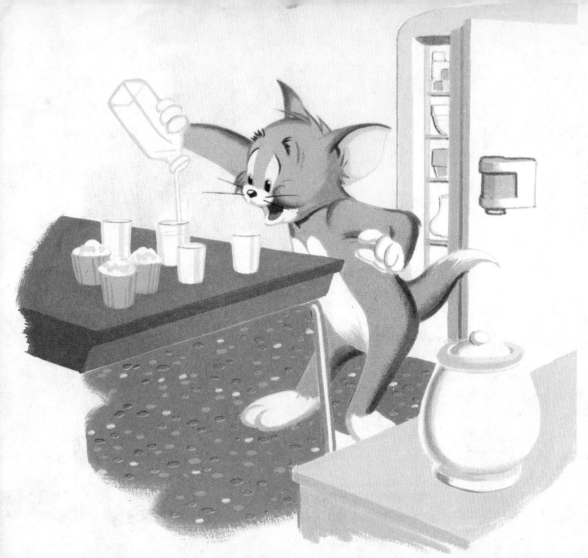

Cook hadn't noticed that the icebox door was open. But Tom Cat had.

"This is the night for a party!" he chuckled.

As soon as Cook had left, he brought out cupcakes and cream from the icebox.

When the food was ready, Tom scrambled up to a
pantry shelf. He brought down streamers left over
from a New Year's Eve party. Humming gaily, Tom
decorated the kitchen.

"Now to hand out invitations!" he said, when he
had finished.

Quickly Tom Cat ran out into the dark night and down to the house of the Fiddler Cat.

"Fiddler Cat, Fiddler Cat," he called. "I'm having a party. Come and bring your fiddle."

From the house of the Fiddler Cat Tom ran on to the house of Yellow Melisande. From the house of Melisande he ran on to the houses of all his friends.

By the time Tom Cat turned back home, six happy cats were trotting along behind him.

Soon the party was in full swing. The Fiddler Cat
played his fiddle. Yellow Melisande stood beside him
and sang.

"A cat's life is the life for me-e-e," she sang. "Meow, meow, it's wild and free-e-e."

The other cats danced to the music and cast hungry looks at the cupcakes.

Somebody else was watching the cupcakes, too.
Jerry and Tuffy stood at the door of their mousehole.

"Look at all that food, Tuffy," Jerry said hungrily.
"Let's go get some of it!"

As softly as could be they skittered up onto the
table, and pounced on the cupcakes.

"Hey!" Tom Cat cried. "Thieves! Thieves! Stop them! Stop them!"

Just then they heard heavy steps coming toward the kitchen.

"It's Cook!" Tom Cat whispered. "She's back early!"

Jerry leaped off the table. He ran to Tom and pulled at his paw.

"In there!" he urged, pointing to his mousehole.
"Hide the cake in there!"

The cats whisked the cupcakes and cream off the table. Pushing and pulling, Jerry and Tuffy squeezed them through the mousehole door.

The footsteps came nearer and nearer. Tom flew
around the kitchen. "The bunting!" he cried. "Take
down the bunting!"

Cook started to open the door. The Fiddler Cat
dove into the waste-basket.

Yellow Melisande leaped into the washing-machine.

A third cat squeezed herself behind the door.

And two little kittens hid trembling in the market-basket.

When Cook came in, there was only Tom, lying
sleepily under the kitchen table.

"Land sakes!" said Cook. "I thought I heard a noise! Must have been my imagination!"

And with a shake of her head, she left again.

"Coast's clear!" whistled Jerry.

The cats came creeping out of their hiding places.

"Ahem!" said Tom to Jerry. "I suppose now you intend to keep all those cupcakes?"

Jerry threw out his chest and looked noble. "Certainly not!" he answered. "Who am I to spoil a party?"

Behind his paw he whispered to Tuffy, "We couldn't have eaten all those cakes alone anyway."

So the party started again, gayer than ever. The Fiddler Cat played, Melisande sang. And in the middle of the floor danced Jerry and Tuffy, each with a big crumb of cake in his paw.